An Alien World

By Julie Haydon

Illustrations by Daniel Atkinson

T0342751

Contents

The Tune of the Tulips

"Ready to disembark, Jack?" Caitlin asked through her communicator.

"Ready," Jack replied.

It was the year 2097. The airlock door of the spaceship closed swiftly behind the explorers as they stepped outside. At that moment, they got their first real look at the newly discovered planet Mystique.

"There's absolutely no sign of Marc," Caitlin groaned, scanning the landscape for their missing crew member, who had failed to return from a solo mission.

"Let's start searching here," Jack said, indicating a field of strange plants. Some were tall with blue tulip-like heads; others were much shorter with grasping purple tendrils.

3

As Caitlin and Jack forced their way through the dense growth, they found themselves in an unusual situation. The tulip plants swayed and moved in an eerie manner and the grasping tendrils of the purple plants unfurled and tried to grab them.

Suddenly Caitlin and Jack heard a high-pitched tune coming from the tulip plants. As the plants hummed, their large blue petals opened, revealing clusters of red fruit.

"Look," whispered Caitlin, as a flock of small unusual birds appeared overhead.

Drawn in by the tulips' song, the birds flew down to feast on the fruit. Just as they landed, one of the purple plants shot out a long tendril. The tulips screamed a warning, but it was too late. The tendril wrapped around one of the little birds and pulled it towards the purple plant's gaping mouth.

"Squaaaark!" screeched the little bird, looking pleadingly at Caitlin and Jack. At once they rushed over and managed to free it.

Recovering quickly, the bird circled Caitlin and Jack, calling to them.

"I think it wants us to follow it," exclaimed Caitlin.

To their amazement, the bird led them to Marc, who was lying a short distance away trapped in a mass of tightly wound purple tendrils. He was semi-conscious and barely breathing.

Hurriedly, Caitlin freed him, while Jack unrolled the jet-propelled stretcher from his backpack. They helped Marc onto the stretcher and began the trek back to the spaceship. To their relief, the birds flew overhead guiding them in the right direction and, at the same time, distracting the purple plants.

"Thank you," Jack called gratefully, when they reached the safety of the spaceship, and the birds flew off into Mystique's pale watery sky.

Reading Science Fiction

Science fiction authors write about how they imagine science and technology to be in the future, in space, or in another dimension or reality. Some people enjoy reading this type of fiction, while others do not.

Science fiction is not usually set in the present day or in the world we know. Some people find science fiction stories exciting. They like to imagine what life could be like in a different time or world.

Science fiction is often full of science and technology. Some of it is real, but a lot of it is imaginary.

There are descriptions of advanced machines and technology, such as spacecraft and space suits. Sometimes the plots are about how science and technology might affect people in the future, which fascinates some readers.

Some science fiction is about aliens living on spacecraft or on other planets, such as Mars. Many people who like to use their imagination enjoy reading about other worlds and life forms.

But many people do not like to read science fiction. They may not be interested in stories that feature a lot of science. Or they may prefer to read fiction set in the real world, because it is more believable.

Some people prefer to read about other realistic people, places and animals, because it allows them to find out more about the world around them.

These people usually prefer stories about characters they can relate to who are involved in everyday experiences.

What people read is a matter of personal choice. If people enjoy reading about different worlds, aliens and science, then they should read science fiction.

But if people prefer more believable characters and settings, they should read other types of fiction.